JUAN HAS THE JITTERS

ANETA CRUZ

ILLUSTRATIONS BY MIKI YAMAMOTO

North Atlantic Books
Berkeley, California

Published by
North Atlantic Books
Berkeley, California

Printed in Canada

Cover art by Miki Yamamoto
Cover design by Jasmine Hromjak
Book design by Happenstance Type-O-Rama

Juan Has the Jitters is sponsored and published by the Society for the Study of Native Arts and Sciences (dba North Atlantic Books), an educational nonprofit based in Berkeley, California, that collaborates with partners to develop cross-cultural perspectives, nurture holistic views of art, science, the humanities, and healing, and seed personal and global transformation by publishing work on the relationship of body, spirit, and nature.

North Atlantic Books' publications are available through most bookstores. For further information, visit our website at www.northatlanticbooks.com or call 800-733-3000.

Library of Congress Cataloging-in-Publication Data

Names: Cruz, Aneta, author. | Yamamoto, Miki, illustrator.
Title: Juan has the jitters / by Aneta Cruz ; illustrations by Miki
    Yamamoto.
Description: Berkeley, California : North Atlantic Books, [2020] |
    Audience: Ages 4–8 years. | Audience: Grades 2–3. | Summary: Juan is an
    autistic boy about to start school, and the thought is giving him the
    jitters; he copes by concentrating on routine things and clapping, but
    he is worried about being laughed at in school—but his teacher has come
    up with a series of math games and made Juan the judge to help him cope
    with his anxiety about the new situation.
Identifiers: LCCN 2020011533 (print) | LCCN 2020011534 (ebook) | ISBN
    9781623174941 (hardcover) | ISBN 9781623174958 (ebook)
Subjects: LCSH: Autistic children—Juvenile fiction. | Anxiety in
    children—Juvenile fiction. | Adjustment (Psychology)—Juvenile fiction.
    | First day of school—Juvenile fiction. | Mathematics—Juvenile
    fiction. | CYAC: Autism—Fiction. | Anxiety—Fiction. | First day of
    school—Fiction. | Schools—Fiction. | Mathematics—Fiction. | Hispanic
    Americans—Fiction. | LCGFT: Picture books.
Classification: LCC PZ7.1.C793 Ju 2020 (print) | LCC PZ7.1.C793 (ebook) |
    DDC [E]—dc23
LC record available at https://lccn.loc.gov/2020011533
LC ebook record available at https://lccn.loc.gov/2020011534

1 2 3 4 5 6 7 8 9 FRIESENS 24 23 22 21 20

Juan marked an X on his calendar.

Tomorrow's the big day!

The school's athletic games!

He clapped.

But he wasn't excited.

Juan clapped to get the Jitters out. They made his tummy *SWOOSH* and *SWIRL*. They BUZZ—BUZZ—BUZZZED in his ears.

The Jitters came when there were too many people, too much noise, and too many changes in his routine. Juan liked every day to be the same.

To calm himself, Juan lined up his books by size.

He clapped.

He sorted his blocks by color.

He clapped again.

He named all the shapes he could find in his room.

CLAP

CLAP

CLAP.

Finally, after he counted the wheels on his toy cars, the Jitters went away.

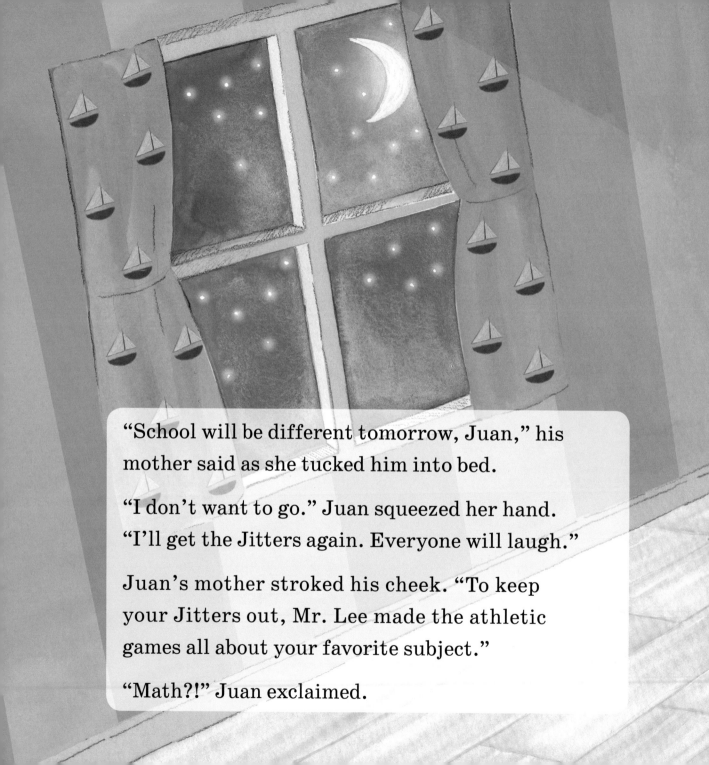

"School will be different tomorrow, Juan," his mother said as she tucked him into bed.

"I don't want to go." Juan squeezed her hand. "I'll get the Jitters again. Everyone will laugh."

Juan's mother stroked his cheek. "To keep your Jitters out, Mr. Lee made the athletic games all about your favorite subject."

"Math?!" Juan exclaimed.

His mother nodded.
"And he picked YOU
to be the judge!"

The next morning, Mr. Lee led Juan to the corner of the soccer field where his classmates waited.

Juan clapped.

"Welcome to Griffith Academy's First Mathletic Games!" Mr. Lee announced. "Please line up."

CLAP—CLAP—CLAP.

Juan tried to soothe himself by looking at the students on the field.

How many came to compete?

Who is tallest?

Who is shortest?

"Are you ready, Mathletes?" Mr. Lee asked.

"Yes!" they shouted.

Juan clapped.

"We'll start with the Sorting Game," Mr. Lee said. "To move on to the next round, sort these blocks by color."

"Ready, set—" He nodded at Juan.

"Go," Juan muttered then

CLAP—CLAP

as Mr. Lee clicked the stopwatch.

To keep calm, Juan focused on the blocks.

What colors are the blocks?

How many groups of colors are there?

Then he judged.

How many students move on to the next round?

"Next, the Matching Game!" Mr. Lee said.

"To make it to the next round, find objects that match these shapes." He looked at Juan. "Ready—"

"Set, go," Juan said.

Mr. Lee clicked the stopwatch just as Juan's palms touched in a quiet

CLAP.

Juan looked around.

What shapes are on the cards?

What objects match the shapes on the cards?

Who made a mistake?

He took his time judging.

"Finally, the Racing Game!"
Mr. Lee announced the last
round. "Pick your wheels."
He gave Juan a checkered flag.

"Ready, set, go!"
Juan shouted.

He eagerly watched as the Mathletes raced to the finish line. His Jitters were gone, but he was the judge, so he counted anyway.

Which one has the most wheels?

Which one has the fewest wheels?

Is there anything with no wheels?

Who is first, second, third?

After Juan announced the winners, Mr. Lee shook his hand. "Thank you for being a fair judge, Juan," he said. "I knew I could count on you."

The Mathletes gathered around Juan. They clapped and chanted, "Juan is number one! Juan is number one!"

Juan smiled. He was too excited to mind the noise.

And, though he didn't have the Jitters, he joined in with a loud

CLAP—CLAP—CLAP,

CLAP—CLAP—CLAP.

ANETA CRUZ is a pre-K teacher and children's book author. She holds a credential in early childhood special education, a BA in English literature, and an MFA in creative writing. When she's not reading, writing, or eating Nutella by the spoonful, she teaches her class of preschoolers how to love books (and other things) as much as she does. She divides her time between the Czech Republic and Southern California, where she lives with her husband, two children, and Poe, the cutest ugly dog in the world.

MIKI YAMAMOTO has been drawing since a very early age. Most of her childhood was spent in her room sketching, coloring, and painting to entertain herself. She studied illustration at Cal State University, Long Beach and has worked for Hallmark Cards, Disney, and Amscan Party. Miki has won numerous awards as a children's book illustrator. She resides in Southern California with her wigglebutt Aussie, Bella.